William Dean Howells

A Sea-change, or, Love's Stowaway

A Lyricated Farce in Two Acts and an Epilogue

William Dean Howells

A Sea-change, or, Love's Stowaway
A Lyricated Farce in Two Acts and an Epilogue

ISBN/EAN: 9783744766074

Printed in Europe, USA, Canada, Australia, Japan

Cover: Foto ©Andreas Hilbeck / pixelio.de

More available books at **www.hansebooks.com**

A SEA-CHANGE

OR

LOVE'S STOWAWAY

𝔄 𝔏𝔶𝔯𝔦𝔠𝔞𝔱𝔢𝔡 𝔉𝔞𝔯𝔠𝔢

IN TWO ACTS AND AN EPILOGUE

BY

W. D. HOWELLS

BOSTON
TICKNOR AND COMPANY
211, Tremont Street
1888

RAND AVERY COMPANY,

ELECTROTYPERS AND PRINTERS,

BOSTON.

CONTENTS.

A SEA-CHANGE.

ACT İ.

LOVE'S STOWAWAY.

SCENE. — *The promenade-deck of the steamer Mesopotamia, two days out from Boston. It is morning, before break-fast. A group of sailors are hauling at a sheet ; and a sail is seen rising, with an audible clucking of the tackle.*

CHORUS OF SEAMEN.

If I had a sweetheart, and she was a rover,
    Haul away, boys, haul away!
I'd follow her all the wide world over,
    Haul away, boys, haul away!

If she said yes, I never would leave her,
    Haul away, boys, haul away!
If she said no, I would go and grieve her,
    Haul away, boys, haul away!

For the will of a girl there is never any knowing,
  Haul away, boys, haul away!
She would want me to stay if she saw me going.
  Haul away, boys, haul away!

Then, never say die; keep a stiff upper lip, boys;
  Haul away, haul, haul away!
The wind is fair, and we've got a good ship, boys,
  Haul away, haul, haul away!

(*The Seamen straggle forward over the deck, singing. Then*
  THERON GAY *steals from the door of the smoking-room,*
  peering fearfully about him.)

THERON, *recitative.*

A surmise or suspicion,
I know not which to call it,
Possesses me, that, without my intending,
I am this very moment emulating
The resolute behavior
Of the heroic and ideal lover
Whose bold philosophy has been indicated
In the soul-stirring accents of the chorus.

Four nights ago, sitting among the flowers
In Mr. Vane's conservatory,

I told my love to Muriel his daughter.
With what result will doubtless be conjectured
When I have added that I took my passage
By the first steamer I could get for Europe
Early the following morning.

And now, there are circumstances
Which lead me to imagine
That Muriel, flying from my hated presence,
Has taken passage on this very steamer.
Such is the simple and probable situation !
But, since we started, we have all been sea-sick,
And hardly any of us has been able
To leave his state-room ;
And it has been impossible to make certain
Of what may be at last a mere conjecture.
Yet now I can no longer bridle
My wild impatience,
And I will ask the first of the ship's people
Whom I encounter ;
And *apropos* of that, just as it happens
Always upon the stage at such a juncture,
When they would hold the mirror up to nature,
Here comes the very man, above all others,
Who can relieve my mind.

(*The* Deck-Steward *appears with a waiter, and a tumbler of lemonade on it.*)

I will accost him.

Steward !

STEWARD.

Yes, sir. Beg your pardon, sir?

THERON.

What's this? The sea's like glass; the ship's as steady as a rock; nobody's sick this morning, surely?

STEWARD, *confusedly.*

You're quite right, sir. It's — it's the force of 'abit, sir. I'm so used to bringin' lemonade to the ladies stretched about 'ere on deck in hevery hattitude of hagony, that I just came hup this mornin', sir —

THERON, *sternly.*

Without the surgeon's orders? What do the rules and regulations say, which are printed, glazed, and framed, and hung up in all the state-rooms?

STEWARD, *dropping on his knees, and extending his waiter imploringly, from which* THERON *mechanically takes the lemonade, and drinks it, setting back the empty glass.*

Don't report me, sir! It was merely the force of 'abit.

THERON, aside.

Now, whether, having got him in my power,
'Twere better throw myself upon his mercy,
And tell him all,
Or rather try *finesse*,
And lead him on,
He knows not how or whither,
To tell me what I wish?
I have an inspiration;
And, as might naturally be expected
Under the unexpected circumstances,
It takes the lyric form; and I will sing it.

THERON, — An Inspiration.

Victim of what box soever,
  Wait and think a little, pray,
Ere the last frail tie you sever,
  Binding you to silence! Stay,
  Do not give yourself away!

If the simple world believes you
  Wiser, richer, better, say,
Than you are, although it grieves you,
  Do not undeceive it! Stay,
  Do not give yourself away!

If you have upon your conscience,
  Sins that struggle to the day,
Stay! Confession would be nonscience;
  (So pronounced for the rhyme's sake, pray!)
  Do not give yourself away!

If your note falls due to-morrow,
  And your heart sinks in dismay,
Try to beg or steal or borrow,
  Ere you own you cannot pay.
  Do not give yourself away!

If you adore some lovely being,
  And you long to tell her, stay,
Since there can be no foreseeing
  That she will not answer nay!
  Do not give yourself away!

If, in short, the cards are shuffled,
  So that you hold but deuce or tray
In life's game, with front unruffled
  Wait, and let your opponent play.
  Do not give yourself away!

THERON, *aside.*

I cannot say just whence this inspiration
Came, and some precepts in it
Certainly strike me as being rather lurid.
I might go on considerably farther ;
But I have said enough already
Quite to decide me not to tell this steward
Aught of myself, but rather seek to pump him.
  Steward !

STEWARD.

Beg your pardon, sir ?

THERON.

For the present I will spare you. And now,
can you tell me — (I must manage this with
great subtlety, so as to throw him off his guard)
— if there is a Miss Muriel Vane of Boston on
board ?

STEWARD.

Well, that, sir, is a question which I can honly
hanswer in one way, sir.

THERON.

How is that ?

STEWARD.

In a haria, sir.

THERON.

What is a haria?

STEWARD.

Haria?   Why, haria is the Hitálian for hair, sir.

THERON.

Hair?

STEWARD.

Yes, sir; in a hair, sir.   A song, sir.

THERON.

Of course.   I expected you to do that.   People always do.   Well?

STEWARD, — *Haria.*

I am a simple deck steward,
Life has left me to leeward!
    I am hold, I am gray,
    I am sad, well-a-day!
But my 'eart shall be hopen to youward.

Welcome were sixpence or shilling;
Ready the 'and, sir, and willing;
   Yet the truth must be told,
   Though for touch of the gold
The palm may be throbbing and thrilling.

THERON.

And what am I to infer from this oracular
rubbish?

STEWARD.

I 'adn't quite finished, you know, sir.

   I cannot be quite explicit
   As to the fact you'd elicit.
     There's so many aboard,
     If I wentured the word,
I might 'it, and again I might miss, it.

That is, I can't say positively, sir. Most of the
ladies 'as kept their berths, sir. Sh! Somebody
comin', sir.

THERON.

Then, I must conceal myself! It is the only
way.

(He re-enters the door of the smoking-room. From the door of the saloon gangway appear two maids, carrying shawls, rugs, and wraps of every kind, with pillows and cushions; MRS. VANE with a Willoughby pug and smelling-bottle; and MR. VANE with a foot-stool, a sun-umbrella, and a steamer-chair. He wearily places the chair, and the maids arrange the wraps and cushions about it, while the old people advance and sing.)

MR. AND MRS. VANE.

Two long days and nights of dread commotion,
   Tossing on a couch of sleepless anguish,
Victim of the wild unresting ocean,
   We have seen our hapless daughter languish.

(They take hands, and chassez gravely, with a dignified dancing-step. The maids, having finished their work, sing sotto-voce, looking over the shoulders of MR. and MRS. VANE.)

THE MAIDS.

Two long days and nights of whim and notion,
   Twisting, turning, scolding, crying, fretting,
We have seen her a perpetual motion
   Of unreal wants and vain regretting.

(They make a saucy dancing-step on each side of the old people.)

MR. AND MRS. VANE.

He who would persistently adore her,
　　When he might have seen she could not pity,
Left her with no choice but flight before her
　　From her country and her native city.

(They dance as before.)

THE MAIDS.

Spoiled and selfish thing, we hope 'twill please her,
　　Now she's left her true and faithful lover.
We should have been willing, just to tease her,
　　If it had been rough the whole way over.

(They dance as before.)

MRS. VANE.

Have you finished, Mary?

MARY.

Yes'm.

MRS. VANE.

Is every thing ready, Sarah?

SARAH.

Quite ready, ma'am.

MRS. VANE.

I feel as if nothing had been done for the poor child, after all. *What* have we done, Matthew?

MR. VANE.

We have secured the captain's room for her.

MRS. VANE.

Well?

MR. VANE.

We have secured the purser's room for ourselves, so as to be constantly near her.

MRS. VANE.

Well?

MR. VANE.

We have secured the seat on the captain's right at table for her.

MRS. VANE.

Well?

MR. VANE.

We have secured the exclusive attendance of the head stewardess.

MRS. VANE.

Well?

MR. VANE.

We have secured the whole time and services of the assistant surgeon.

MRS. VANE.

Well?

MR. VANE.

In short, as nearly as possible, we have secured the entire ship in every way.

MRS. VANE, *sighing.*

It seems very little.

MR. VANE.

It *is* very little, but it's all we could do.

MRS. VANE.

Well, let us go and see if Muriel can be persuaded to come up. Oh, when I think of what the child has undergone! And all from that wretch! And all for nothing!

MR. VANE.

Well, my dear, I have cheerfully joined you in censuring the young man in song and dance; but I really can't see that he was so very much to blame. He is a person of respectable standing in society.

MRS. VANE.

Yes.

MR. VANE.

He was graduated at Harvard with three honors: Reading, Writing, and Arithmetic, I believe they were.

MRS. VANE.

Yes.

MR. VANE.

He is very talented, with an ambition to shine as the scholar in politics.

MRS. VANE.

Yes.

MR. VANE.

To this end he has already secured a position on a Sunday paper as reporter, with a salary of ten˙ dollars a week. It is not a vast sum ; but, having a great deal of our own, we naturally despise money in others.

MRS. VANE.

Yes.

MR. VANE.

As such things go, he is in the way to promotion. In less than twenty-five years he might hope to be an Own Correspondent, with fifteen dollars a week.

MRS. VANE.

Yes.

MR. VANE.

He is a person of unblemished character and exceptionally pleasing manners. In dress he is a gentleman, — an American gentleman of English pattern.

MRS. VANE.

Yes.

MR. VANE.

He was very much in love with Muriel; and it is customary with young men to tell their love.

MRS. VANE.

But wholly unnecessary! *All* the young men were in love with Muriel, but none of them thought it necessary to tell it. Why should *he ?*

MR. VANE, *with conviction.*

True !

MRS. VANE.

He might have seen how sensitive, how high-spirited, how delicately constituted she was, how little calculated to know her own mind.

MR. VANE.

Very true !

MRS. VANE.

He might have known that it would be extremely repulsive and completely prostrating.

MR. VANE.

I see.

MRS. VANE.

But he was not even satisfied with telling Mur:el that he loved *her*.   He insisted upon knowing whether she loved *him*.

MR. VANE.

That was certainly going too far.

MRS. VANE.

The child had no alternative but flight, and — here we are !

MR. VANE.

Perfectly true !   He was obviously wrong.   But what should he have done?

MRS. VANE.

He should have waited.

MR. VANE.

Waited?

MRS. VANE.

Yes.

MR. VANE.

What for?

MRS. VANE.

For — for a more fitting opportunity.

MR. VANE.

Oh! How long?

MRS. VANE.

Indefinitely. Women sometimes have to wait all their lives. Why shouldn't men?

MR. VANE.

There's a great deal in that.

MRS. VANE.

Muriel is not exacting. Gratify her wishes, few and simple as they always are, and she asks nothing more. But come, Matthew! The child will be distracted at our absence. What are you stopping for?

MR. VANE.

Oh, nothing! Merely an appropriate little ode that I thought I might repeat. But no matter!

MRS. VANE.

Is it *very* appropriate?

MR. VANE.

Quite.

MRS. VANE, *with resignation.*

˜ Perhaps you had better repeat it, then. You would never feel easy if you didn't.

MR. VANE.

I think you are right, my dear.

MR. VANE, — *A Little Ode.*

There was a youth,
  He loved a maid.
He spoke the truth,
  She fled affrayed.

Had he forborne
  A little space,
Fate might have worn
  Another face.

In later mood
  It might have fared,
That she had wooed,
  And he been scared!

MRS. VANE.

I don't think any thing of the kind would have happened with Muriel.

MR. VANE.

Very possibly.　I merely throw out the suggestion.

MRS. VANE.

Yes, it has a very plausible sound; but it's much more probable that she would never have wooed him.

MR. VANE.

You think not?　But why?

MRS. VANE.

Because, in that case, there would have been no opera.

MR. VANE.

That hadn't occurred to me.

MRS. VANE.

Well, come now!　Muriel will be *so* impatient!

(*As the* VANES *go below,* THERON *dashes from his concealment, and clutches the* STEWARD *by the arm.*)

THERON, *wildly.*

Who — who — is this young lady?

STEWARD.

What young lady, sir?

THERON.

Don't trifle with me! The one who is coming
up.

STEWARD.

The one who 'as taken the captain's room?

THERON.

Yes! Her name!

STEWARD.

I 'aven't 'appened to 'ear 'er name, sir: but I
'ave a list of the cabin-passengers 'ere in my
pocket, sir; and if you'll kindly 'old this waiter a
moment, sir, I'll read it for you.

THERON, *taking the waiter.*

Be quick! I am of a very impulsive nature, though trained in the school of indifferentism at our leading university; and I may not be able to restrain my impatience.

STEWARD.

All right, sir! I've got it! 'Ere it is! I won't keep you a moment, sir. (*Unfolding the list.*) Perhaps you would like to 'ave me sing it, sir?

THERON.

Do you ordinarily sing it?

STEWARD.

Well, yes, sir, we do, sir, on this ship, sir. The Mesopotamia is one of the *new* Retarders, you know, sir.

THERON.

Very good, then! I should much prefer you to sing it.

(*He takes a shilling from his pocket, and gives it to him with a great show of secrecy, which the* STEWARD *emulates in receiving it.*)

STEWARD.

Thank you kindly, sir. You won't forget the pound ten at the hend of the voyage, *will* you, sir? Let me see a moment, sir. Oh, yes! "List of saloon-passengers per steamship Mesopotamia, sailing from Boston to Liverpool, April 1, 1884.

" Mr. Julian Ammidown.
   Mr. and Mrs. Rufus Brown.
   Major Connelly.
   Colonel Donnelly.
   Mrs. Susan Dewell.
   Dr. Jacob Ewall.
   Mr. and Mrs. Follansbee.
   Mrs. 'Arris, Miss 'Arrises (three)" —

Goin' hout to heducate 'er daughters in Paris, and leavin' Mr. Haitch to supply the funds at 'ome, I suppose.

THERON.

It is the national custom. Go on.

STEWARD.

All right, sir.
   "Mr. Ingham and Mr. Jones" —

THERON.

No, no! Stop! I thought I could bear it for the sake of the effect, and the resemblance to Leporello's list in Don Giovanni; but I can't. Skip the rest of the alphabet, and get down to the V's at once!

STEWARD.

" Mr. and Mrs. Matthew Vane " —

THERON.

O my heart, burst not in twain!

STEWARD.

" Miss Muriel Vane, two maids and pug. Rev. Dr. Silas Wrugg."

THERON, *dropping the waiter.*

Wait! Stop! Hold on! It is she! I knew it as soon as I recognized her parents' voices in my place of concealment.

STEWARD, *starting back.*

Then you are —

THERON.

A stowaway !

STEWARD.

Very sorry, sir ; but I shall be obliged to report you.

(*He picks up the fragments of the tumbler, and replaces them on the waiter.*)

THERON.

Report me ! And after I have spared *you* ?

STEWARD.

Well, you see, sir, a stowaway is very different, sir. The rules are very strict about reportin' 'em, sir. You'll be put in hirons, and sent back from Liverpool by the first return steamer.

(*He winks, and wags his hand behind him for money.*)

THERON.

Irons? Are you open to bribery?

(*The* STEWARD *turns round, wagging his hand.* THERON *continues aside.*)

And am I the slave of this corrupt person? Subject to the beck and call of a deck steward?

A thought strikes me !   (*Aloud.*)   But I am not
a common stowaway, — not one of those pitiful
wretches, who, dying of poverty and homesickness
in a foreign land, basely seek to return to friends
and country at the expense of the company.   My
passage has been fully paid, and I occupy Berth
81 on the saloon-deck.   Listen, and I will tell
you all.   I —

STEWARD.

I beg your *pardon*, sir !

THERON.

Well?

STEWARD.

I *beg* your pardon, sir; but don't you think
you'd better sing it?   It's rather more the custom,
sir.   I *beg* your pardon !

THERON.

Of course.   I ought to have thought of that
myself.

STEWARD.

It would be a little more in keepin', sir.   A
great many gentlemen 'ave confided their 'eart

'istories to me, sir; and they halways sung them, sir. Many's the 'alf crown I've 'ad from them, sir, for listenin'.

THERON, *giving him money.*

Very well.

(*He sings.*)

I am Love's Stowaway —

•

STEWARD, *interrupting.*

I *beg* your pardon, sir; but don't you think you'd better wait for the chorus? It's just comin' hup, sir. The lookout 'as sighted a hiceberg, and the chorus is comin' hup to see it.

THERON.

• But I thought I heard a chorus at the beginning of the piece.

STEWARD.

So you did, sir. That was the Chorus of Seamen. We've got two choruses on the Mesopotamia. The hold boats honly 'ad one. *This* chorus is a Chorus of Passengers.

THERON.

Oh, well! if it's a chorus of *saloon*-passengers —

STEWARD.

It is, sir.

THERON.

Then, I don't mind waiting a reasonable time for them; but they mustn't be long.

STEWARD.

They won't keep you a moment, sir.   'Ere they come now, sir.

(*Enter* CHORUS OF PASSENGERS, *singing by groups.*)

GROUP OF GENTLEMEN PASSENGERS.

We are lawyers and physicians,
Bankers, brokers, electricians,
Publishers and politicians,
Editors, professors, students
Of all kinds, whom our imprudence,
    In the mad pursuit of wealth,
Has compelled, for relaxation,
To endure a brief vacation;
    And we all are going over for our health.

But whatever be our station,
Our profession or vocation,
Our politics, our objects, our ideals, and the rest,
Love alone, and love supremely,
Love alone, and love extremely,
   Is our life's great interest!

ALL.

Yes, our life's great interest!

GROUP OF FASHIONABLE LADIES.

We are daughters, wives, and mothers
To these gentlemen and brothers,
Whom, with very many others,
Our expensive tastes and passions,
Our caprices and our fashions,
   Goaded in pursuit of wealth;
But, worn out with the enjoyment
Which has formed our sole employment,
   Now we all are going over for our health;
And whatever be the notion
Of womanhood's devotion
   To such objects and ambitions as have our souls
     possest,
Love alone, and love supremely,
Love alone, and love extremely,
   Is our life's great interest.

ALL.

Yes, our life's great interest!

GROUP OF MERCHANTS RETURNING FROM THE BOSTON
FOREIGN EXHIBITION.

Russians, Polacks, Turks, Armenians,
Hindoos, Arabs, and Athenians,
Chinese, Japs, and Abyssinians,
Germans, Frenchmen, and Egyptians,
Orientals of all descriptions,
   From the mad pursuit of wealth,
In the city of the Yankees,
Hardly richer ev'n in Thank'ees,
   We are flying homeward for our health.
But whatever be the fraction,
Division or subtraction,
   Of the general sum-total as in numerals exprest,
Love alone, and love supremely,
Love alone, and love extremely,
   Is our life's great interest.

ALL.

Yes, our life's great interest!

GROUP OF SHOP-GIRLS.

We are some of the sales-ladies —
Minnies, Mamies, Susies, Sadies —
From the famous house whose trade is

The distinction and the glory
Of all modern retail story;
   And from its abundant wealth,
As a novel advertisement
Of ingenious devisement,
   It is sending us all over for our health.
But whatever were its motive,
A business one or votive,
   In despatching us so unexpectedly upon this quest,
Love alone, and love supremely,
Love alone, and love extremely,
   Is our life's great interest.

ALL.

Yes, our life's great interest!

ALL THE LADIES.

But we see no iceberg!

STEWARD.

It's pretty low down yet, ladies. (*To* THERON.) Now's your time, sir! I told you they wouldn't be long, sir!

THERON, *giving him money.*

I shall never forget your thoughtful kindness in procuring me this sympathetic audience.

ONE OF THE LADIES, *recitative.*

And who, pray, is this gentleman we see here, —
With us, although apparently not of us?

THERON.

Ladies, if you will allow me, I will introduce
myself.

THERON, — *A Confession.*

I am Love's Stowaway!
  Love lured me from my home,
  And far across the wandering foam
He bade me stray.

I am Love's Stowaway!
  He chose the fated bark:
  And, darkly plotting in the dark,
He did betray.

I am Love's Stowaway!
  And, where my love was hid,
  I followed blind, as blind Love bid:
I must obey.

I am Love's Stowaway!
  And here my love and I
  Together from each other fly,
The self-same way!

(THERON *is about to continue his song, when enter* MURIEL
with her father and mother, maids and pug.)

ONE OF THE CHORUS, *recitative.*

Wait! Stop! Excuse the seeming interruption!
We think the lady wishes to say something.

MURIEL, *recitative.*

Merely to make a personal ·explanation,
Such as, in good society, is usual
On mingling with a company of strangers.

MURIEL, — *A Statement.*

I am a member of that Aristocracy,
  Wholly composed of the lovelier sex,
Which, in the heart of our New-World Democracy,
  Reigns, the observer to please and perplex.

Since I was born, well, I do not think, really,
  That I have been of the least use on earth:
All has been done that could *be* done, ideally,
  Utterly useless to make me from birth.

Never a wish that was not at once gratified;
  Nothing refused me that money could buy;
All my opinions respected and ratified,
  Since I could utter the first in a cry;

Flattered, deferred to, obeyed in society
   Like a young princess come into her own;
Free to do all that I would to satiety;
   Law to myself, first and last, and alone;

Dressed like one born to the purple imperial;
   Housed like a duchess, and served like a lord;
And, like the heroine of a cheap serial,
   By all that looked at me wildly adored;

I am a member of that Aristocracy,
   Wholly composed of the lovelier sex,
Which, in the heart of our New-World Democracy
   Reigns, the observer to please and perplex.

And the great wonder is, not that I'm odious —

CHORUS OF ALL THE MEN.

No, we don't think you so! Nobody could!
No, we make protest in accents melodious!

MURIEL.

Thanks. You are all, I am sure, very good.

Well, then, the miracle is, that the wealthily
   Born and conditioned American girl,
Placed, as to all things that spoil, so unhealthily,
   Never's the Oyster, but always the Pearl.

(*She sinks into her steamer-chair, where the two maids elaborately arrange her.* THERON *stealthily retires toward the door of the smoking-room, and the* CHORUS *gradually withdraw.* MURIEL *remains with her party and the* STEWARD.)

MRS. VANE.

How do you feel now, dear?

MURIEL.

So much better, mamma, thank you. How nice the air is! Mamma!

MRS. VANE.

Yes, dear?

MURIEL.

Would you mind just looking in my jewelry-case for poor Carlino's best collar? He's so shabby in this old thing!

MRS. VANE, *kissing her.*

I'm *so* glad to see you taking an interest in life again. I'll be back instantly.

[*Exit.*

MR. VANE.

Are you sure you're perfectly comfortable, my child?

MURIEL.

Oh, perfectly, papa! Papa!

MR. VANE.

Yes, my child?

MURIEL.

I hate to be so much bother; but there's no
one else I could trust to bring me — let me see!
— my other earrings. I put on these drops never
thinking, and diamonds are shocking before break-
faşt. (*She takes them out, and hands them to
her father.*) It's too bad, sending you, papa!

MR. VANE.

My child (*kissing her*), you know how happy
it makes me to do any thing for you.

[*Exit.*

MURIEL.

Sarah !

SARAH.

Yes, Miss Muriel?

MURIEL, *taking a bracelet from her wrist, and giving it to* SARAH.

I've been a great deal of trouble to you. Here's a little thing — I know you admire it. I've seen you looking at it.

SARAH.

O Miss Muriel! what shall I do? (And me been saying such awful things about the poor, dear, pretty creature!)

MURIEL.

Nothing, please. Sarah!

SARAH.

Yes, Miss Muriel?

MURIEL.

Do you suppose you could — wait a moment till I can think. Oh! — find me a lighter handkerchief? This is so heavy! It fatigues me.

SARAH.

Why, Miss Muriel, I'd jump overboard for you!

[*Exit.*

MURIEL.

Mary !

MARY.

Yes, Miss Muriel?

MURIEL, *taking a brooch from her neck, and hand-
ing it to her.*

Don't thank me, please.   And — Mary !

MARY.

Yes, Miss Muriel?

MURIEL.

Do you think you could go away, and stay a
little while, without any particular excuse?   It's so
tiresome making them !

MARY.

Why, of course I can, Miss Muriel.   And you're
the sweetest, sensiblest, untroublesomest young
lady in *this* world !   And I won't come about the
whole day again !

[*Exit.*

MURIEL, *with a sigh.*

Now, Steward, we are alone. Have you any first name?

STEWARD.

Why, miss, I 'aven't 'ardly any *last* name. I'm Robert, miss.

MURIEL.

Well, Robert, I can see that you have a heart.

STEWARD.

I 'ave, miss. *Hall* the stewards on the Mesopotamia 'as 'em, miss. The captain, and the hofficer on duty, and the 'ole crew, 'as 'em. 'Earts, and electric lights, set bowls, and annuncihators in all the state-rooms. Any little thing I could bring you, miss?

MURIEL.

No, Robert, not at present. I have no appetite.

STEWARD.

But your happetite will come back now. You won't be hill any more. Was you pretty bad, miss?

MURIEL.

The sea-sickness was the least part of it (*sighing*) ; though I *was* sick. Yes. But, Robert!

STEWARD.

Yes, miss?

MURIEL.

What were all those people doing here when I came up?

STEWARD.

It was honly the chorus of passengers, miss, who 'ad come hup to see the hiceburg.

MURIEL.

Oh! And who was the young. gentleman who appeared to be singing to them?

.

STEWARD.

Why, he was tellin' hall about 'imself, miss, in the song.

MURIEL.

Oh, I dare say! But you never can make out the words, and I had no libretto. (*After a mo-*

ment, musingly.)   There was something strangely familiar in his voice and figure. But, of course, it could not be.

MURIEL, — *A Misgiving.*

I must not, I dare not, imagine it he,
  In his love and his sorrow forsaken ;
Though, if we were not such a distance at sea,
  I should say that I was not mistaken.

The form and the face were the same ; but, ah, me !
  Divided by many a billow,
I make my moan to the pitiless sea,
  And he sighs under the willow.

My moans cannot reach him, my love, where he sighs
  In metaphor under the willow :
The voice of his sorrow inaudible dies,
  Where I toss on the wandering billow.

But I thought for a moment — a breath, — it might
    be
  That I really was not mistaken,
Although such a very great distance at sea,
  In my pride and my folly forsaken.

He sang very well, I fancied.

STEWARD, *with musical reluctance.*

Well, honly tolerable, miss. We've 'ad a great many tenors on the Mesopotamia.

MURIEL.

Yes; but his voice had a certain sympathetic quality, — a *brio*, a *timbre* —

STEWARD.

Very true, miss; but it was very thin in the hupper notes.

MURIEL.

Oh, it wasn't perfect, I suppose! Do you happen to know his name, Robert?

STEWARD.

Well, no, miss, I don't know 'is *name:* but I've got my list of the passengers 'ere; and if you'll kindly 'old my waiter, miss (*he gives it to her, with the fragments of the tumbler on it*), I'll read it hover to you.

MURIEL.

You are very good, Robert.

STEWARD.

Or, what do you say, as you seem to be a connyshure, miss, to my singin' it?

MURIEL.

Do you sometimes sing it?

STEWARD.

Yes, miss, I *generally* sing it.

MURIEL.

I shall be delighted.

STEWARD, *singing.*

" Mr. Julian Ammidown.
  Mr. and Mrs. Rufus Brown.
  Major Connelly.
  Colonel Donnelly.
  Mrs. Susan Dewell.
  Dr. Jacob Ewall.
  Mr. and Mrs. Follansbee.
  Mrs. 'Arris, Miss 'Arrises (three) " —

Oh! Beg your pardon, miss! 'Ere's a name I missed once before between the Hefs and the Haitches, —

" Mr. Theron Gay " —

MURIEL, *flinging the waiter from her, and bursting wildly from her chair, with her hands to her temples.*

Theron !

THERON, *rushing from the door of the smoking-room.*

Muriel !

(*They fly into each other's arms, and sing.*)

MURIEL AND THERON, — *A Collision.*

MURIEL.

Oh, if you be some fond and dear illusion,
    Some blessed dream,
Born of the brain's fantastical confusion,
    Be what you seem !
            Stay with me, stay,
            Fade not away,
Oh, dearly loved illusion !

THERON.

I am no vision, no hallucination :
    Be not afraid !
Wholly unchanged in substance and formation,
    I could not fade,

My love, my bride,
Ev'n if I tried,
Like an hallucination!

MURIEL, *with dignity.*

Then, if you are really Mr. Theron Gay, of Boston, Mass., I must ask you, as a gentleman, to leave me.

THERON, *astounded.*

Leave you, Muriel? But you just requested me to remain!

MURIEL.

That was under the impression that you were a pleasing unreality. I was very explicit.

THERON.

And, as a reality, am I so unpleasing?

MURIEL.

That is not the question. You must release me.

THERON.

If you insist. But why?

MURIEL.

For one thing, it is essential to the plot.

THERON, *releasing her.*

Oh! if it is essential to the plot, of course I must yield. The literary instinct teaches that.

MURIEL.

And, besides, you have no right to be here. You had no right to follow me. Especially on the same steamer.

THERON.

But, my love, I didn't know you were on board. That is the strangest part of it. I fled, in my madness and despair, by the first steamer I could get. It happened to be the very ship you had embarked in. (*Tenderly.*) Cannot you recognize some design of Fate in this coincidence, Muriel?

MURIEL.

If it is, as you say, purely an accident —

THERON.

Oh, it is!

MURIEL.

Then I forgive you, but on condition that you go ashore instantly.

THERON.

Why, but, Muriel —

MURIEL.

Don't reply! I simply ask you, as a gentleman, to go ashore, and not persist in attentions which you must see are very disagreeable. (*She returns to her steamer-chair, and talks while he makes her comfortable in it with the shawls, cushions, and wraps.*) I will not ask you how it is that you came to choose this ship —

THERON.

It was a fatality. Will you have this shawl over your feet?

MURIEL.

Yes, thank you. And I will not imply that you knew very well I was on board.

THERON.

Oh, I swear to you that it would be doing me serious injustice! I had scarcely any idea of it. (*Fitting a cushion to her shoulders.*) Is that comfortable?

MURIEL.

Perfectly, thanks. I will not insinuate that you have been planning this interview ever since you knew I was here, helpless and defenceless.

THERON.

Oh, never! Will you have the pug in your lap, or in your arms?

MURIEL.

In my arms, please. You are very kind, I'm sure, and I'm quite ashamed to give you so much trouble; but I will merely say, that, if you have a spark of honorable feeling, you will go ashore at once. I will be calm, I will be reasonable; but you must go.

THERON.

Why, but, Muriel, it's quite impossible! We are forty-eight hours out from Boston; and, even at the comparatively low rate of speed characteristic of the Retarders, we must be two or three hundred miles at sea. I would do any thing to oblige a lady, any thing to gratify my dearest love; but, at the moment, I find it quite impracticable to go ashore.

MURIEL.

You will not?

THERON.

I cannot!

MURIEL.

Then, I shall simply go wild.

MURIEL, THERON, STEWARD, — *A Delirium.*

Yes, I shall go wild!
Befooled, beguiled,
Followed afar in my flight by insolent treason,
I call, with the last ray of reason,
Papa!
Mamma!
Come to your child!

THERON.

No, do not go wild:
You are not beguiled!
Hear me, my loved one, my only one, listen to
reason!
I am wholly guiltless of treason.
Papa!
Mamma!
Come to your child!

STEWARD.

They both will go wild.
He, unjustly reviled,
Cannot convince her that he is guiltless of treason,
Cannot make her listen to reason.
Papa!
Mamma!
Come to your child!

(MR. *and* MRS. VANE *rush distractedly on deck, with the* CHORUS OF PASSENGERS, *all bringing life-preservers.*)

MR. VANE.

Mamma!

MRS. VANE.

Papa!

BOTH.

We come to you, child!

CHORUS.

Papa!
Mamma!
Come to your child!

MRS. VANE.

Oh! what is it, my precious one?

MR. VANE.

My child, what is it?

CHORUS.

Is it an iceberg?

> (*They get out their opera-glasses.*)

THERON, *with exasperation.*

No: it is an ice girl!

CHORUS.

A nice girl?

THERON.

Yes, an ice girl!

CHORUS.

Oh, no puns!
We are not the ones
To be amused with trivial word-play of that kind.

THERON, *furiously.*

I said a girl of ice,
Not a girl that is nice.
To any sort of jesting I am not now inclined.

MURIEL, *clinging to a hand of each.*

O papa! O mamma! See! It's Theron!

MRS. VANE, *putting on her glasses.*

It is indeed! Wretch! How came he here?

MR. VANE, *putting on his glasses.*

Upon my word, so it is. Mr. Gay, you must be aware that this is very — very —

MRS. VANE.

Use some violent expression, Matthew!

MR. VANE.

I will, my dear, — unexpected!

THERON.

I know it, Mr. Vane. It's quite unintentional.

MRS. VANE.

Oh! Unintentional!

MURIEL, *faintly.*

Don't be harsh with him, mamma. But when

I simply asked him, as a gentleman, to go ashore, and leave me —

MRS. VANE.

He refused?

MURIEL.

He said he couldn't.

MRS. VANE.

A likely story! Where is the captain? I will see the captain about this. (*Running, and shaking her parasol at the man at the wheel.*) Oh — ah! My good man!

MAN AT THE WHEEL, *looking round.*

Ay, ay, ma'am!

MRS. VANE.

Where is the captain?

MAN AT THE WHEEL.

He's down in the boiler-room, ma'am, takin' the reck'nin'.

MRS. VANE.

Send him here at once.

MAN AT THE WHEEL.

Ay, ay, ma'am !

(Recitative down speaking-tube)

Captain, you're wanted here ! And I may hadd,
    sir,
Seems a young lady, taken wery bad, sir.
I can't just tell you if there's need to worry,
But the young lady's mother says to 'urry.

(The CAPTAIN *appears on deck instantly, with a sextant in
    his hands, a telescope under one arm, and a speaking-
    trumpet under the other.)*

CAPTAIN, — *An Explanation.*

I am the Mesopotamia's very obliging commander;
    And I will say it, with whom boasting was never
        the wont,
No swifter craft than this has swum the seas since
        Leander
    Executed his famed feat on the dark Hellespont.

No, the Mesopotamia is not an old-time Retarder,
    • Such as we read of once in the American press,
Flabby and flat in *cuisine,* and frowsy in state-room
        and larder,
    With (as in classical art) nothing at all in excess.

Passengers here may converse with officers on and
off duty,
And will especially, please, talk with the man at the
wheel;
Honor, obscurity, riches, poverty, homeliness, beauty,
Constitute equal parts here of the same common-
weal.

Such are the company's rules; and I think you will
easily gather
From my behavior thus far, that the particular part
I would assume toward you all, is the part of affec-
tionate father,
With the more delicate ones' interests chiefly at
heart.

Well, ladies, which of you sent for me?

MRS. VANE.

It was I, captain, on behalf of my daughter.

MR. VANE.

On behalf of our daughter — yes!

CAPTAIN.

And what can I do for you, miss?

MURIEL.

Nothing. But the man at the wheel makes me giddy, turning it round so.

CAPTAIN, *through his trumpet, to the* MAN AT THE WHEEL.

Lash your wheel!

MAN AT THE WHEEL, *obeying.*

Ay, ay, sir! (*Attempting to sing.*)
   I am the —

CAPTAIN, *sternly.*

Belay that! (*To* MURIEL.) Any thing more, miss?

MURIEL.

No, — only the ship seems to tremble a good deal.

CAPTAIN, *to the* MAN AT THE WHEEL.

Tell the officer on duty to send me the engineer.

MAN AT THE WHEEL.

Ay, ay, sir! (*Down speaking-tube.*) Engineer!

(ENGINEER *appearing instantly, and attempting to sing.*)
   I am the —

CHORUS.

Oh, stow it!
We know it.

CAPTAIN.

We've had enough of explanation, and we'll show it.

CAPTAIN, — *A Suggestion.*

If you wish to deliver some long explanation,
   Mainly in honor and praise of yourself,
Be not deceived with the fond expectation,
   That the world, which it brings neither glory nor
      pelf,
         Will list to your call:
   The right way for you is to hire a hall!
         Yes, hire a hall!

If your tongue should be long, and be hung in the
      middle,
   And it chance that you be of the lovelier sex,
With a gift beyond symphony, cymbals, or fiddle,
   The soul of your husband to pierce and to vex,
         And you *must* caterwaul,
   The right way for you is to hire a hall!
         Yes, hire a hall!

If you are a poet, and lately have written
  Some verses you fancy uncommonly fine;
If you are a lover, just given the mitten, —
  And no one will hearken, you should not repine.
    'Tis the fortune of all;
  The right way for you is to hire a hall!
    Yes, hire a hall!

If you're a pianist, and have a fell passion
  For banging away at the keys by the hour,
Allow me! There is a more merciful fashion
  Than socially making displays of your power, —
    A fashion for all:
  The right way for you is to hire a hall!
    Yes, hire a hall!

If you are a statesman or ward politician,
  A man with a grievance, a maid with a grief,
An agent, a dentist, a soul with a mission,
  Beware how you turn to your friends for relief.
    I'll be frank with you all:
  The right way for you is to hire a hall!
    Yes, hire a hall!

If you are a —

CHORUS.

Oh, hire a hall!

CAPTAIN.

I bow to the will of the -- Remnant. (*To the* ENGINEER.) Go down, and stop the engines.

ENGINEER.

Ay, ay, sir !

[*Exit.*

CAPTAIN, *to* MURIEL.

Is that all, miss?

MURIEL, *reluctantly.*

Y-e-e-e-e-s.

MRS. VANE.

Muriel, *I* must speak, if *you* will not. Captain, she is annoyed by the presence of one of the young gentlemen on board, who refuses to go ashore.

CAPTAIN.

Which young gentleman is it, ma'am?

MRS. VANE.

Shall I indicate him more particularly, Muriel?

MURIEL, *veiling her eyes with her hand.*

I suppose you must, mamma. But don't be harsh !

MRS. VANE.

I will be firm. It is Mr. Gay.

CAPTAIN, *to* THERON, *sternly.*

I have not had the pleasure of seeing you before, sir, I think.

THERON.

Very true. I have lately been describing myself in song to the ladies and gentlemen present as Love's Stowaway. So far as relates to the payment of my passage, the term is not perfectly accurate. The purser will tell you that my ticket was quite regular. I occupy Berth 81 on the saloon-deck ; but I called myself Love's Stowaway because I was here without the knowledge of a young lady who was flying on your ship from a hemisphere which my attentions had rendered insupportable to her. I will not spare myself, sir —

MURIEL, *to* MRS. VANE.

Oh, how generous, how magnanimous, he is !

MRS. VANE.

Hush, my child! If you give way, the affair must end here.

MURIEL.

Well, I will be patient, then.

THERON.

I will not shrink from saying that I told her my love at a moment when it was surprising, and perhaps painful, to her. I also fled; and, by a series of accidents, I found myself on the same ship with Miss Vane. If you had been on deck immediately after the opening chorus, you could have heard me state the same facts in recitative. Now, do with me as you will. I am, strictly speaking, Love's Unintentional Stowaway. But I am a stowaway, and I do not shrink from the penalty. Put me in irons.

MRS. VANE, *to* MURIEL, *who is weeping.*

Remember, if you yield now, you spoil every thing.

CAPTAIN.

Well, ma'am, there are practical difficulties in

the way of Mr. Gay's going ashore. I have just been taking an observation in the boiler-room, and we are twenty-three miles from land. It is a very quick run : we are only two days out.

MURIEL.

But, captain, you could turn the ship round, and go back with him, couldn't you?

CAPTAIN.

Yes, miss, we could do that ; but it would postpone our arrival in Europe almost indefinitely. It would be simpler to throw him overboard.

MURIEL.

I don't think I could quite consent to that. It would be inhuman, wouldn't it?

CAPTAIN.

It would be unusual ; but, as I understand, it is an extreme case.

MURIEL.

Yes, it is. It is very provoking. Is there no other way?

CAPTAIN.

Yes. If you could wait, miss, we might transfer him to the first homeward-bound ship we met.

MURIEL.

Perhaps we had better wait.

CAPTAIN.

In the mean time I will just have him loaded with chains.

MURIEL., *starting forward.*

With chains?

CAPTAIN.

Yes, miss, as a stowaway by his own confession.

MURIEL.

Oh, yes! (*She sinks back in her chair.*) Of course!

THERON, — *A Defiance.*

Yes, load me with chains!
  What are your iron links
To the bonds in which my last hope wanes,
  My spirit sinks?

Yes, load me with chains! ·
    Spare not, do not delay!
Soon I shall lie, 'neath the suns and the rains,
    Death's Stowaway!

(*A group of Seamen appear with handcuffs and heavy
chains. At the end of each stanza they dance some steps
of the Sailor's Hornpipe.*)

THE SEAMAN'S PROTEST.

Oh! don't you think it's hard on the sympathetic
    sailor,
    Whose heart is in his hand, and whose hand is
        on his hip,
To make him play the part of policeman or of
    jailer,
    And render him detestable to all aboard the ship?

For our natural disposition we refer you to the pic-
    tures,
    And the story-books the landsmen write about the
      · jolly tar;
Though we might make, of course, our suggestions
    and our strictures,
    You must go to them, if really you would know
      us as we are.

'Tis our ordinary habit to sing of Sue and Polly
  As we lightly climb aloft, to reef the topsail in
    the gale;
We are all opposed, on principle, to care and mel-
  ancholy;
  We love to catch the shark, and harpoon the
    sleeping whale.

Then, when all the toils and dangers of the day
    are safely over,
  'Tis our custom to lie basking before the fo'c's'le
    fire,
Spinning yarns and piping ditties of maiden and of
    lover,
  And watch the cheery flames till they flicker and
    expire.

And nothing more repugnant to the feelings of a
    sailor,
  Than loading of a gentleman with chains can be
    conceived;
And that we should have to play the policeman
    or the jailer
  On this ship's, a thing that none of us would
    ever have believed.

    (*They load* THERON *with chains.*)

MURIEL, *sobbing convulsively.*

But, captain, suppose we don't meet any home-ward-bound ship?

CAPTAIN.

Then, miss, — the idea has just occurred to me, — we could put him off on an iceberg. We are now entering the region of floating ice, and we may encounter a suitable iceberg at any moment. They are continually drifting toward the coast of Labrador; and the chances are, that within a week, or ten days at the farthest, he would find himself within the Straits of Belle Isle, from whence he could easily make his way by the Intercolonial Railway to Halifax, and so by boat to Boston.

MURIEL.

Do you think an iceberg is preferable to a homeward-bound merchant-vessel?

CAPTAIN.

It's about an even thing, miss.

MURIEL, *thoughtfully.*

It would be more romantic on an iceberg.

CAPTAIN.

Yes, it would certainly be more romantic.

MURIEL.

I should think Theron would prefer it. Well, then, let it be whichever we meet first.

CAPTAIN.

All right, miss. Steward!

STEWARD.

Yes, sir?

CAPTAIN.

Tell the third officer in charge of the passengers' luggage to have Mr. Gay's boxes brought up out of the hold; and go and fetch his valise out of his state-room yourself. Not a moment is to be lost.

STEWARD.

Yes, sir.

[*Exit.*

(*A derrick is seen lifting* THERON'S *trunk through a bulkhead in the deck. The* STEWARD *re-appears with* THERON'S *bag and travelling-shawls. The latter removes his Glengarry cap, and puts on his silk hat, as if going ashore. The* CHORUS, *now fully realizing the horror of the situation, start forward in protest.*)

CHORUS.

What is this, O dread commander
  Of the Mesopotam-i-a?
If we rightly understand her,
  We are filled with wild dismay.

In default of home-bound vessel,
  Would she see her true-love, pray,
Left with the winds and waves to wrestle,
  On an iceberg cast away?

CAPTAIN.

Yes; for, if I understand her,
  She will brook no more delay.

MURIEL.

Only because, O dread commander!
  You can think of no other way.

THERON.

Yes, fond friends and sympathizing,
  Truly there is no other way
In the scope of our surmising;
  And, as a gentleman, I obey.

MR. VANE.

This is politeness most surprising.

MRS. VANE.

It is the least that he could say!

MR. VANE.

Were I readier at devising,
He should never be cast away.

STEWARD.

I am worse by the thirty shilling
   'E would have given me, I dare say,
At the hend of the voyage!

CHORUS.
                        Thrilling,
   Far beyond our feeble lay,
Is the existing situation.
   No one, we think, will say us nay,
When we add an execration
   Of the Fates that still betray.
But since nothing can be more certain
   Than that there seems no other way,
Dropping over our grief a curtain,
   Let us be light, let us be gay!

(*They dance.*)

CAPTAIN, STEWARD, AND MR. AND MRS. VANE, *dancing together.*

Let us be light, let us be gay!

THERON, *dancing alone.*

Let them be light, let tnem be gay!

MURIEL, *keeping time with her head.*

Let him be light, let him be gay!

But in the mean time, Theron, if you have any thing to say in justification of your strange conduct, I cannot refuse to hear it; though, of course, it won't affect the final result.

THERON.

No, Muriel, I understand that perfectly. Do you mean my conduct in finding myself on the same ship with you?

MURIEL.

No: that is all past, now!

THERON.

Oh! Then, you mean my conduct in offering myself to you. Well, there is nothing I would

like to say; but there is something I would like
to sing.

MURIEL.

Could you make it short? I am really quite
worn out. I have been so *terribly* sea-sick,
Theron! And I haven't literally slept a wink
since I came on board. Singing seems to string
the ideas out so! And there has been so much
of it! And then, if there happens to be an
encore, there's no living through it.

THERON.

I will try to boil it down.

MURIEL.

Do! And I hope the music isn't abrupt or
dramatic? I really couldn't bear it, in my ex-
hausted state.

THERON.

No: it's a simple, pleasing air, — rather soothing, than otherwise, I believe.

MURIEL.

Well, then, sit down by me while you sing,

Theron, and take my hand in yours. We may
part so soon !

(*He obeys.*)

THERON, — *A Justification.*

You ask me why? We both were young;
   And round our lives the rosy air
Full of divine expectance hung,
   Like the soft light that everywhere
   Clings to the leafless branches bare,
   In March while yet the trees are bare.

You ask me why? It was the time
   The bird begins to build its nest,
And all the world is filled with rhyme
   Of soul to soul, and breast to breast;
   With rapture wild, and sweet unrest,
   With spring-time's wild and sweet unrest.

You ask me why? It was the hour
   When Doubt is lulled, and Hope awakes,
And certain tender dreams have power
   Upon us for their own sweet sakes;
   And all such different seeming takes,
   Such mystic midnight seeming takes.

You ask me why? It was the place
   Of many a summer-breathing flower;
The rose's bloom, the lily's grace,
   Drooped o'er us in the mimic bower,
   Around the fountain's gush and shower,
   The tiny fountain's gush and shower.

You ask me why? We sat alone.
   In distant rooms we heard the waltz
Throb dully; and, in undertone,
   You bade me tell you of your faults;
   Amid the pulses of the waltz,
   You bade me tell you of your faults.

(*While he sings, she drowses, unseen by him. Her head
   sinks on her breast.*)

THERON.

Muriel, love? She weeps!

CHORUS.

No, no, she sleeps!
The aching heart, the weary brain,
At last are free from pain.
   Muriel sleeps.

MR. AND MRS. VANE.

Yes, yes, she sleeps!
Be silent, oh! and make no stir,
Lest you awaken her.
Muriel sleeps.

CAPTAIN, *through his trumpet.*

Ay, ay, she sleeps!
The wretch who dares to breathe a word
Henceforth, goes overboard.
Muriel sleeps.

MAN AT THE WHEEL, *sounding the whistle.*

Ay, ay, she sleeps!
Oh, softly, whistle, softly sigh
The news afar and nigh!
Muriel sleeps.

THERON.

Oh, joy! She sleeps!
It was my song that brought surcease
Of pain to her, and peace.
Muriel sleeps.

MURIEL, *stirring in her sleep.*

Come back! *I* love you too!

CHORUS OF ALL THE VOICES.

Hush, hush!
Our Muriel dreams.
A tender flush
Bepaints her cheek, and seems
The light of dreams.

Hush, hush!
Our Muriel raves.
Oh, cease your roar and rush,
Ye winds and waves!
Our Muriel raves.

Hush, hush!
Of love she raves,
And parting; and a gush
Of hot tears steals
From underneath her fallen lids, and laves
Her pale, worn cheeks,
And eloquently speaks
The sorrow that she feels,
Even while she sleeps!
Even while she sleeps,
She weeps!

(*The scene is slowly darkened until all the figures become in-
visible, while the* CHORUS *continues.*)

CURTAIN.

ACT II.

MURIEL'S DREAM.

(*The scene is the same ; but the deck is now gorgeously deco-
rated with rich stuffs in various colors, hanging from the
shrouds and yards, and forming a pavilion, open at the
back, so as to show the other guard of the steamer, and
the sea beyond. The front of the house is wreathed with
flowers, enormous rosettes adorn all the upright surfaces,
the masts and funnels are likewise garlanded, and the
mouths of the funnels are filled with vast bouquets, through
which the smoke is seen escaping. There is a touch of
something fantastic in all these decorations, and in the
dress of all the persons present, who are in ball-costume.*)

CHORUS, *promenading arm in arm.*

    Ladies and gentlemen,
    If at all singular
    In our appearance
      Some of us seem,

80

Let us enlighten you:
We are not really
People, but only
   Things in a dream, —
   Muriel's dream!

All this magnificent
Paraphernalia .
That you will notice
   Here, if you please,
Is but the scenery
That quite subjectively,
As in a vision
   Dreaming she sees, —
   Muriel sees!

And though the opera
May appear tedious
In its performance,
   Yet it is plain
All its occurrences
Are simultaneous,
All in an instant
   Flashed on the brain, —
   Muriel's brain!

MURIEL, *magnificently dressed, promenading arm in arm with* THERON.

And so we're going to have a ball! How perfectly fascinating! Do you know, Theron, I've often wondered they didn't have them oftener on the Retarders? It would certainly be an attraction.

THERON.

Yes, I think it would. How do you like the decorations?

MURIEL, *pausing a moment to glance up at them, with her hands clasped through his arm.*

Beautiful! A little peculiar, perhaps?

THERON.

No: I don't think so.

MURIEL.

Well, perhaps not. Who did them?

THERON.

They were designed by the Society for the Prevention of Decorative Art. The piano is from the establishment of Messrs. Chickerway & Steining. (*He pauses, and takes up in his hand a toy grand piano.*)

MURIEL.

Oh, yes! It's one of their new Baby Grands. But (*regarding it critically*) isn't it rather small?

THERON, *walking on.*

It *is* small; but it will grow.

MURIEL.

Oh, certainly! It will grow — in time.

THERON.

Yes: it will grow old.

MURIEL.

That was what I meant. There are to be refreshments, I suppose?

THERON.

Well, very light. *Bouillon* for the ladies, and chocolate-creams and chewing-gum for the salesladies.

MURIEL.

Perfect! Who suggested the ball?

THERON.

Why, to tell the truth, *I* thought of it.

MURIEL.

But how came you to have such a fortunate inspiration? You're so stupid, usually, you know. (It doesn't seem to be quite what I meant to say !)

THERON.

Well, I don't know. I thought it would be a graceful little attention to the steerage-passengers if I got up a sort of *fête* for them in celebration of my approaching departure.

MURIEL., *fondly*.

How *like* you, Theron ! But (*looking about*) I don't see any of the steerage-passengers here.

THERON.

No : they're rather a low set. Of course we couldn't have them present.

MURIEL.

Of course not. Theron !

THERON.

Yes, dearest?

MURIEL.

I never thought! But where did the flowers come from? So far at sea, you know.

THERON.

Oh! The flowers are artificial.

MURIEL.

Why, so they are! But they looked as unnatural as the real ones.

THERON.

The captain has them watered with cologne from time to time, and that keeps them fresh. Here comes the man, now.

(*A seaman appears with garden-hose, and sprinkles the flowers, executing, at the same time, some steps of the Hornpipe.*)

MURIEL.

I never saw any thing so lavish! And how characteristic of a seaman, to dance!

THERON.

The captain has spared no expense, and the crew all enter into the spirit of the affair.

MURIEL, *with an uneasy sigh.*

I suppose the decorations are all right; but don't you think the company is rather queer?

THERON.

I see nothing queer about them.

MURIEL.

Well, if I didn't know that I was awake, I should certainly think I was dreaming. Those Arab gentlemen, now: they seem to have become quite dark since I first saw them.

THERON.

Yes, they are Arabian Nights now.

MURIEL.

That accounts for it. Well, it must be right. But why do the gentlemen all keep their bonnets on?

THERON.

To prevent the bees in them from escaping.
They've got bees in their bonnets, to a man!

MURIEL.

I see. Theron!

THERON.

Well?

MURIEL.

I don't like to ask so many questions, but *why*
has the captain got on an over-skirt?

THERON, *carelessly*.

Oh! I suppose he's heard of the secretary of
the treasury issuing a steamboat-captain's com-
mission to that lady in Mississippi, and wishes to
be ready for the change.

MURIEL.

How stupid of me not to think! But *do* you
like papa in mamma's fichu?

THERON.

I think it's rather becoming.

MURIEL, *thoughtfully.*

Perhaps the color is. But now — mamma in a dress-coat ! Do you think it's quite the thing?

THERON.

Why, it's very common, you know.

MURIEL.

Yes. What have they *all* got on?

THERON.

Their life-preservers.

MURIEL.

Oh ! I see. But is it safe, having them round the knees?

THERON.

Well, they do less harm there, probably. They can take them off if any thing happens.

MURIEL.

True. Why have they got all these signs stuck about, " Keep off the grass "? I don't see any grass.

THERON.

No : it isn't up yet. But there'll be plenty of it before we get to Liverpool, — sea-grass, you know. The Mesopotamia is generally covered with it when it comes into port. It's very decorative.

MURIEL.

I dare say. I would like to speak with the steward, please.

STEWARD, *instantly appearing, with his left hand developed into a spacious waiter.*

Yes, miss?

MURIEL, *staring.*

Ugh ! Oh ! I merely wished to see the captain a moment. Robert !

STEWARD.

Yes, miss?

MURIEL., *indicating his hand.*

Is it — comfortable?

STEWARD.

Perfectly, miss. It's convenient; and it can't fly hout of your 'old in rough weather, miss, like the hold style of waiter.

MURIEL.

Yes, there's that to be said. And — Robert!

STEWARD.

Yes, miss?

MURIEL.

You don't notice any thing odd about the company, do you?

STEWARD.

Nothing whatever, miss.

MURIEL., *in bewilderment.*

Yes: that's what Theron said. Well, send me the captain. (*The* STEWARD *vanishes, and the* CAPTAIN *appears.*) Oh! I have been waiting for you. But (*severely*) I wish you wouldn't flash upon me in that disagreeable manner. One would think you were something at the theatre, coming up out of the floor.

CAPTAIN.

Well, miss, I'm greatly pressed for time. I've to get this ball over before breakfast.

MURIEL.

It seems to me it's a very droll time for a ball.

CAPTAIN.

It's a *matinée;* to let the steerage-passengers go to their work in season. Besides, I dare say you've been at a great many balls where you had to hurry to get through before breakfast.

MURIEL.

That is perfectly true. But now tell me frankly, captain, do you notice any thing strange about your guests?

CAPTAIN, *looking round.*

Well, no, miss. They seem dressed as people usually are at a dancing-party.

MURIEL., *in despair.*

Oh, dear! But Theron, now: why does The-

ron wear that enormous bow on the small of his
back? Whisper it, please.

CAPTAIN, *glancing from* THERON *to the pug, which
is similarly equipped, and then replying through
his trumpet.*

Because the other one has it, I suppose.

MURIEL, bursting into tears.

Oh, don't turn the poor fellow into ridicule at
the last moment ! It's inhuman ! (*She runs to
him, and, detaching the bow, flings it into the sea.
Then a thought seems to strike her.*) Theron !

THERON.

Yes, Muriel?

MURIEL.

Why, you are still here !

THERON.

Yes. We haven't met any home-bound vessel
yet.

MURIEL.

Well, it won't do. We have made all our
preparations for parting, and we must part.

MURIEL AND THERON, — *Duet of Resignation.*

MURIEL.

Yes, we must part, for parting comes to all :
  It is the thought that poisons love's delight ;
In rapture's cup it is the drop of gall ;
  At noon it is the shadow of the night.

THERON.

Yes, we must part. We only live to part :
  The bird must leave its native sky afar,
The leaf its bough, the rose its stem, the heart
  Its hope ; the day must lose its morning star.

BOTH.

Yes, we must part, O love ! or soon or late,
  Whether we laugh or weep, or smile or sigh,
It is of all that lives the common fate ;
  And love itself at last must fade and die.

MURIEL, *sobbing.*

But what about the iceberg, Theron? The
captain promised me, that, if we met no home-
bound vessel, you should be put off on an iceberg !

THERON, *sobbing.*

The lookout hasn't sighted any iceberg yet.

LOOKOUT, *on top of the house.*

Sail, ho!

CAPTAIN, *through his trumpet.*

Where away?

LOOKOUT.

On the port-quarter, sir.

CAPTAIN.

Heave to!

LOOKOUT.

Ay, ay, sir!

CAPTAIN.

Cast the log!

LOOKOUT.

Ay, ay, sir!

CAPTAIN.

Reef the starboard watch!

LOOKOUT.

Ay, ay, sir!

CAPTAIN.

Eight bells !

LOOKOUT.

Eight bells it is, sir !

CAPTAIN.

Yare !

LOOKOUT.

Ay, ay, sir !

CAPTAIN.

Luff !

LOOKOUT.

Ay, ay, sir !

CHORUS.

Oh, how excessively
Novel and interesting !
Let us be writing
　　Letters to send —
If he will pardon us
Offering to trouble him
With their conveyance —
　　Home by our friend.

(*They all take out postal-cards, and write.*)

LOOKOUT.

Little mistake, sir!

CAPTAIN.

Well?

LOOKOUT.

It isn't a sail, sir. It's a hiceberg.

CHORUS, *getting out their glasses.*

An iceberg!

THERON.

Muriel!

MURIEL.

Theron!

(*They fly into each other's arms.*)

CHORUS OF ALL THE GENTLEMEN PASSENGERS.

Cruel girl! Can nothing move you
   From the deed that you would do?
If it be worthy death to love you,
   Know that we are guilty too.
   Put us off on the iceberg too!

CHORUS OF ALL THE LADY PASSENGERS.

Shameless thing! If we could only
  Do what we would like to do.
His exile should not be lonely.
  Let these wretches stay with you!
  We would go on the iceberg too.

THERON, *soothing* MURIEL.

Nay, kind ladies, do not chide her:
  She but does what she must do.
·I am willing to abide her
  Final wish in the premises. You
  Must not think of coming too.
  No, kind ladies, it would not do!

MURIEL.

That is very sweet of you, Theron. Not that
I care for them. But I'm sure you won't suffer
much, if any. It's coming summer, and the iceberg will be cool and pleasant. You will be
abundantly provided with food, fuel, cigars, and
reading-matter. You'll soon drift ashore somewhere. But, in any case, it can't be helped.
You must go. There's no other way of getting
rid of you. Don't you see, dearest?

THERON.

Oh, yes! I see, Muriel. You're quite right.
I dare say I shall do very well.

MURIEL.

Captain, we don't seem to be approaching very
rapidly.

CAPTAIN.

That's because we're going *towards* the iceberg.
If we were sailing *from* it, you would see how
soon we should overhaul it.

MURIEL.

Oh, yes! I forgot that this was one of the
Retarders.

(*Sound of distant singing is heard.*)

CAPTAIN.

But, even as it is, we sha'n't be long. There,
you can hear the people on the iceberg already.

MR. VANE.

Are they usually inhabited, captain?

CAPTAIN.

Yes, usually, but not always.

MR. VANE.

How very odd!

MRS. VANE.

And are the inhabitants like us?

CAPTAIN, *with some embarrassment.*

Well, ma'am, that depends upon what you mean by *us*. If you mean *me*, — well, no: they're not precisely like us. They're fairies.

MURIEL.

Fairies?

CAPTAIN.

Yes, miss. And there's another difference. They're all beautiful young ladies. Yes, it's a singular fact, but one well known to science, that the inhabitants of icebergs are all fairies, all young, all beautiful, and all ladies.

MURIEL., *with misgiving.*

O Theron, dear! do you think you'd *better* go?
If any thing should happen to you, I could never
forgive myself.

THERON.

Don't be troubled, Muriel.   I shall be perfectly
safe, I've no doubt.

CAPTAIN.

There, miss, you can hear them quite distinctly
now.

CHORUS OF THE ICEBERG FAIRIES.

(*As they sing, the iceberg approaches; and they are seen
scattered over its peaks and slopes, draped in flowing
white and blue, and wearing fillets of frosted silver in
their hair.   The iceberg softly touches the side of the
steamer, and the seamen make it fast.   They place a
staging from the rail to the deck.*)

Out of the frozen realms of the North,
   From the dreamless solitudes
   Where immemorial silence broods
Over a world that is white and whist

As is the pale, dead moon,
　Singing a mystic rune,
Clad all in pearl and amethyst,
Life out of Death, we have wandered forth.

Out of the beautiful northern sky,
　From the eerie flash and play
　Of lights that fairer than the day
Paint the long night of half a year,
　We may describe ourselves
　As some auroral elves,
Who, having left their normal sphere,
Through the world are wandering far and nigh.

MR. VANE.

This is very interesting, very definite, and, upon the whole, satisfactory. But I'm rather surprised that they should adopt that scientific view of the moon's condition. From fairies I should expect something more poetical.

CAPTAIN.

Oh! science has penetrated everywhere; and I may say that Iceberg Fairies are, as a rule, nothing if not scientific.

MR. VANE, *with conviction.*

True. (*From moment to moment, various inscriptions reveal themselves on the sides of the iceberg, as "St. Jacob's Oil Conquers Pain," "Anti-Fat," "Burdock Blood Bitters," "Rock and Rye," etc.*) I observe that they seem to have adopted several of our popular remedies at the North Pole.

CAPTAIN.

There's a great deal of rheumatism there, and, with an exclusive meat-diet, the blood needs purifying in the spring. You'll find the whole North Pole painted over with patent-medicine advertisements in the American fashion.

MR. VANE.

Ah! that's an additional motive for not discovering it. Well, Muriel, I suppose there's no occasion for further delay. Shall I speak to these ladies, or will you?

MURIEL.

Perhaps *I* had better, papa, as they seem strangers. (*She advances to the rail of the steamer next the iceberg.*) Hmm! Let me see! Whom shall I ask for? Oh! Why, of course! Ladies, can any of you tell me if the queen is at home?

THE ICE PRINCESS, *advancing politely.*

Miss Vane?

MURIEL.

Yes. The Ice Princess?

.

THE ICE PRINCESS, *smiling.*

Yes. Mamma will be *so* sorry to miss you. But she's confined to her cavern with a cold to-day.

MURIEL.

Oh, I'm very sorry! I hope it isn't any thing serious?

THE ICE PRINCESS.

Oh, no! Merely a cold in the head. But, of course, it's trying. Could I give her any message from you?

MURIEL.

You're very kind. I don't know that I ought to trouble you with a business-matter. Er — won't you come aboard?

THE ICE PRINCESS, *complying, with all her fairies.*

Oh, thank you! And I shall be only too glad if I can do any thing for you.

MURIEL.

It's nothing. Merely a young gentleman whom I would like to have you take with you, and put ashore somewhere on the American coast. If you don't actually touch anywhere, it don't matter: he could swim a few miles. I suppose I needn't go into details; but it's quite necessary he should leave the steamer. Theron! (*She extends her hand behind her; and* THERON, *with his travelling-shawl over his arm, and carrying his valise, approaches, and takes it.*) The Ice Princess, Mr. Gay! (*They bow in acknowledgment of the introduction.*) It is Mr. Gay whom I wish to have go with you.

THE ICE PRINCESS, *politely.*

Oh, yes! (*She examines him through her pince-nez as he retires.*) Isn't he rather good-looking?

MURIEL.

Yes, — rather.

THE ICE PRINCESS.

And amiable?

MURIEL.

Yes, — rather amiable.

THE ICE PRINCESS.

Well, you see, we are all ladies, and, mamma not being at all well, do you think it would be very nice?

MURIEL.

Oh, perfectly! There are so many of you!

THE ICE PRINCESS.

That is true. But he is a Harvard man, I suppose; and none of us ever learned Greek.

MURIEL.

Oh! they don't *learn* Greek at Harvard. If you will read the College Fetich, you will see that they only *study* it. I dare say *he* didn't learn *any* thing. (*To* THERON, *who seems to have spoken.*) What? (*To the* ICE PRINCESS, *as if explaining.*) Oh, yes! Athletics, of course, and modern languages, — the german; it's one of those languages that you dance, you know.

THE ICE PRINCESS.

Well, that's very nice.   What are his principles?

MURIEL.

I don't quite understand you.   Do you mean his political principles?   He is a Protectionist.

THE ICE PRINCESS.

We are Protectionists too.

MURIEL., *with fine reluctance.*

Oh !   I don't think he's an extreme one.

THE ICE PRINCESS.

We are moderate too.   We believe in a tariff for revenue ; for we must have pocket-money, you know.   At the same time, we are Protectionists. As ladies, we have to be protected, of course. But I referred not so much to his political principles, as his theories of life.

MURIEL.

I believe, that, at one time, he thought it was hardly worth while.   He had been reading a little of Mallock. But he told me he had got over that in his junior year. He is very earnest now.

THE ICE PRINCESS.

I am glad of that. *We* are very earnest too.

MURIEL.

When you say *we*, do you mean yourself individually, or all the fairies?

THE ICE PRINCESS.

Both. Is he literary, or scientific?

MURIEL.

Scientific, I *think*. At any rate, he's written a novel.

THE ICE PRINCESS.

Oh, indeed! *We* have written novels too. Is he of the old romantic school, with real heroes and heroines, or the modern analytic, photographic school, with just common people?

MURIEL.

I'm sure I can't say: *I* couldn't read it.

THE ICE PRINCESS.

Nobody can read ours either.   Is he sceptical?

MURIEL.

No, indeed !   That's *quite* gone by.   Are you?

THE ICE PRINCESS.

Well, we're rather scientific, you know.

MURIEL.

Why, you might as well — let me see ! — you might as well wear a tie-back as to talk agnosticism *now*.

THE ICE PRINCESS, *thoughtfully*.

I hadn't heard.   Mr. Gay could convert us, perhaps.   And you say his character is irreproachable?

MURIEL.

Quite.

THE ICE PRINCESS, *sighing*.

He is certainly very handsome.   He's been abroad?

MURIEL.

Of course. But he isn't at all Europeanized, if that's what you .mean.

THE ICE PRINCESS.

I m glad of that. Oh! One thing more, please. I hope he isn't a Bostonian. Their manners are so cold. They chill us.

MURIEL.

I shouldn't have thought they could chill *Ice* Fairies.

THE ICE PRINCESS.

They can chill *any* thing. And precisely because we *are* Ice Fairies, we pine for warmth.

THE ICE PRINCESS, — *An Illustration.*

The rose that in some winter room
So frailly grows, so palely blows,
Knows in its heart a brighter bloom,
And longs to be a summer rose, —
In sun and shower, a summer rose.

The song each silent soul within
  That weakly tries, that meekly dies,
For utterance that it may not win,
  From poet-lips would scale the skies, —
  A poet's song would scale the skies.

The love that lurks in every breast,
  So kind a thing, so blind a thing,
If with a smile or word caressed,
  Would wake, and rise, and be a king, —
  Of life and death the lord and king.

MURIEL.

Yes, I admit all that; but it stands to reason,
that, if the manners of the Bostonians are cold,
their hearts are warm. Theron, what should you
say in evidence of the hidden warmth of the
Bostonians? For they certainly *do* hide it.

THERON.

Very little. I know there has been a good deal
of talk about our manners; but I ask, what if we
do seem cold?

MURIEL, *to the* PRINCESS.

Yes, what if we do?

THERON.

We make no pretence of being warm.

MURIEL.

No one could deny that!

THERON.

And that is more than you could say of people whose manner is more cordial.

MURIEL., *fondly.*

O Theron, *be* a popular orator! Be very, very classic! And affective!

THERON.

Muriel, I will! Two or three points have occurred to me; and, if her Highness will give me her attention for a few moments, I think she will admit their force.

THE ICE PRINCESS.

Why, certainly, Mr. Gay. I will listen, with pleasure.

THERON, — *A Rejoinder.*

It is not where the greatest smoke is,
    That the fiercest fire is seen:
It is not where the finest joke is,
    That the longest laugh comes in.

It is not where the winds are coldest,
    That you find the deepest snow:
It is not where the word is boldest,
    That you feel the heaviest blow.

It is not where the surf is loudest,
    That the great sea-serpents hide:
It is not where the throng is proudest,
    That you meet the blushing bride.

THE ICE PRINCESS.

Yes: I see, and it may all be as Mr. Gay says; but we have never had a young gentleman among us yet, and I must take time to think it over.

MURIEL.

There's no hurry. Of course I didn't expect you to decide immediately.

THE ICE PRINCESS.

No. And, while we are thinking, we should like to dance a little ballet, as people always do when any thing important is pending. Perhaps it would amuse you?

MURIEL.

It will be very good of your Highness. Imperial, or royal, by the way?

THE ICE PRINCESS.

Imperial, please. The queen is an empress, you know.

MURIEL.

Oh, yes! Like Victoria. We shall be perfectly delighted to have you dance.

BALLET AND SONG BY THE ICE FAIRIES.

With the tender chords all muted,
Fairy-voiced and fairy footed,
Let us trip, and let us glide,
Gleaming,
Sparkling,
Dreaming,
Darkling,
O'er the ocean's frozen tide.

Down the crystal ice-peaks swarming,
On the crystal ice-field forming,
Let us drift like falling snow,
    Swirling,
        Sweeping,
    Curling,
        Creeping,
Like the lightly falling snow.

Then let silence, deep and hollow,
On our merry uproar follow:
Let us all, like shapes of snow,
    Brightly
        Shimmer,
    Lightly
        Glimmer,
Stop as if all frozen so!
      (*They all stop instantly*)

MURIEL.

How perfectly charming! What do you call it?

THE ICE PRINCESS.

Frost on the Window-Panes. Isn't it a pretty name?

MURIEL.

Lovely! And so significant! I think — if you'll excuse my proposing it — the passengers would like to dance a little now, to show their appreciation and gratitude.

THE ICE PRINCESS.

Oh! we shall be charmed, I'm sure.

BALLET AND SONG BY THE PASSENGERS.

With a burst of music flashing
Lightning-like and thunder-crashing
 On the stilly, startled air,
   Quickly
    Forming,
   Thickly
    Storming,
 Fill the wide deck everywhere!

Swains and nymphs of every nation,
Recking naught of race or station,
 Mingle in the merry dance,
   Widely
    Straying,
   Idly
    Playing,
 Back and forth, retire, advance!

Then, like leaves that whisk and rustle,
When the winds of autumn hustle
  Through the woodlands bare and gray,
        Hither
            Hieing,
        Thither
            Flying,
  Flit and flutter and fleet away!

THE ICE PRINCESS.

Delicious! And what do you call *this*, pray?

MURIEL.

Oh! it's merely a little pastoral. I forget the name. Theron, what do they call this dance?

THERON.

The Grasshopper; or, The United Gayeties Sociable.

THE ICE PRINCESS, *with mortification.*

Why, certainly! I ought to have recognized it. By the way, it reminds me of a little thing of our own, which I should like to have the fairies dance for you if —

CHORUS OF PASSENGERS.

Oh, no ! Miss Muriel would want *us* to dance again, and we've had quite enough of it.

CAPTAIN.

Yes : give us a rest !

CAPTAIN, — *A Demand.*

Give us a rest, for life at best is brief ;
  For life is full of weariness, at best :
Give to the troubled heart and brain relief,
  Give us, with strife and loss and grief opprest,
      Give us a rest !

Nepenthe does not grow on every bush,
  Nor wealth await all young men who go West :
Then, from the world's unending shove and push,
  The idle turmoil, and the useless quest,
      Give us a rest !

From all endeavor to provoke *encores*,
  From plays on words, from puns with wit unblest,
From all the sad variety of bores,
  And hobbies of peculiar interest,
      Give us a rest !

MR. VANE.

Isn't this very much to the same purpose as the song you sang in the first act in regard to hiring a hall?

CAPTAIN.

Yes, it is. But it suggests a less expensive method of relief. Sometimes it costs a great deal of money to hire a hall, but you can simply *stop*, any time, for nothing.

MR. VANE.

I had not looked at it in that light.

CAPTAIN.

Naturally. You have probably never been at sea before.

MRS. VANE.

I hope you're satisfied now, Matthew! Exposing your thoughtlessness before everybody!

THE ICE PRINCESS, *to* MURIEL.

I noticed that Mr. Gay seemed to dance very well.

MURIEL.

He reverses nicely.

THE ICE PRINCESS.

Well, I have thought it all over very seriously, and I have concluded to take him. (*She passes her hand through his arm.*)

MURIEL, *faintly*.

Thank you. Of course you will be kind to him?

THE ICE PRINCESS.

Very kind.

MURIEL.

If he should be homesick —

THE ICE PRINCESS.

I will read to him, or sing; or the fairies will dance.

MURIEL.

And if he should be ill — so far from a doctor —

THE ICE PRINCESS.

We have all the popular remedies. Besides, mamma understands sickness perfectly, — she's ill so much, herself, — and he shall have the best of care.

MURIEL.

And if — if — he should be unhappy? If he should ask — for — for — me?

THE ICE PRINCÈSS, *with dignity.*

I think his interests may be safely intrusted to me, in every way. And it shall be my special charge to see that my husband *doesn't* ask for you. I should like to hear him!

MURIEL., *aghast.*

Your husband! But you're not going to marry him?

THE ICE PRINCESS.

Certainly. In fact, — we Ice Fairies are very frank; perhaps too much so, — I find upon reflection, that I have always loved him.

MURIEL.

You have always loved him? But you have never met him before!

THE ICE PRINCESS.

That makes no difference. Though I'm not so
sure about not meeting him.

THE ICE PRINCESS, — *A Reminiscence.*

Somewhere before our lives began,
Ere I was maid, or he was man,
   Somewhere in shapeless space,
Ideas of what was to be,
But wholly unembodied, we
   Met somehow, face to face.

That he was he, and I was I,
We inly knew, but knew not why,
   Though that we loved we knew:
Something within us or without,
Taught us to feel beyond a doubt,
   That we were one, though two.

And still I feel that nameless thrill
That trembled through me then, and still
   The hope that then I felt.
The strange, dim rapture of that hour,
I feel again its heavenly power,
   I pant, I burn, I melt!

MR. VANE, *interrupting.*

Excuse me, your Imperial Highness, but isn't that rather dangerous —*for you ?*

THE ICE PRINCESS.

What dangerous?

MR. VANE.

Er — melting.

THE ICE PRINCESS.

Not at all. For, if I were to thaw altogether, I should re-form again immediately.· I am a Reformer.

MR. VANE.

Civil Service?

THE ICE PRINCESS.

Certainly !

MRS. VANE.

Of course she is, Matthew ! Don't be absurd !

MURIEL.

Is there any more?

THE ICE PRINCESS.

Only one more stanza : —

And as it once was, æons since,
It shall be ever, æons hence,
  Whether we live or die.
In depths below, in heights above,
To love we live, we die to love,
  We, we ; he, he ; I, I !

For these reasons I propose to marry him at once.

MURIEL, *politely*.

But you must allow us to offer you some refreshments first. They are just coming up.

(*A train of table-stewards, in red and yellow tights and the ordinary stewards' jackets, appears, bearing trays with cups of bouillon, and plates of chocolate-creams, and sticks of chewing-gum. They keep time to a march from Lohengrin blent with Yankee Doodle.*)

THE ICE PRINCESS.

You're *very* kind !

MURIEL.

Theron, what is it reminds one so of Lohengrin? Something about the music —

THERON.

No : that reminds me rather more of our national anthem.

MURIEL.

Or the dress of the stewards —

THERON.

It's the ordinary dress of table-stewards.

(*The stewards serve the bouillon to the passengers.* MURIEL *takes a cup from a tray, and hands it to the* PRINCESS.)

MURIEL.

Will your fairies have bouillon, or some of the chocolate-creams and chewing-gum?

THE ICE PRINCESS.

Oh ! chewing-gum, please. *They* were all sales-ladies once ; and they're very nervous still, poor things !

MURIEL, *looking anxiously round.*

It doesn't seem to be going off very well, Theron. Don't they generally sing at a banquet? It seems to me that they ought to clink their cups of bouillon together, and sing.

THERON.

Yes : I don't see why they don't ! It's very odd.

CHORUS OF LADY AND GENTLEMEN PASSENGERS.

We are keeping our breath to cool our broth.

CHORUS OF FAIRIES AND SALES-LADIES.

How can we sing, with our mouths full of chewing-gum ?

MURIEL, *with pique.*

Oh, very well ! We can't oblige you to sing, of course ; though I think the effect would be better.

THE CHORUS, *clinking their cups, suddenly burst forth.*

A song, a song,
For the brave bouillon,
For the bouillon hot and steaming !
We sing its praise
As our cups we raise,
With bouillon sparkling and gleaming.

Beef-tea, beef-tea,
      The champagne of the sea!
For every sort of weather,
      Or smooth or rough,
      This is the stuff!
Touch again, and drink it together!

MURIEL.

Ah, I thought you would have to do it! Thank you very much, indeed. (*To the* PRIN-CESS.) Well, I have been thinking it over too; and I don't wish you to *marry* Theron. I wish you merely to transport him to the nearest point on the American coast, and — drop him.

MRS. VANE, *severely.*

That is all you are expected to do; and perhaps if you had been as sensitive in regard to others as you profess to be in regard to yourself it wouldn't be necessary to call your attention to a very well-known fact. And, oh! if I had the trump of doom —

STEWARD, *appearing with a banjo in his hand.*

The captain's mislaid the trump of doom, ma'am; but 'ere's the cook's banjo.

MRS. VANE, *examining it.*

Well, the banjo will do very nicely, Robert.
Now, then ! *Con espressione,* please.

(*The* STEWARD *strikes the cadence on the banjo at the end
of each two lines.*)

MRS. VANE, — *An Observation.*

Oh ! never yet in castle-hall or bower
   Was high-born dame, or simple damozel,
That dreamt the banished victim of her power
   Might find another he could love as well.

She ever saw him wandering unconsoled,
   Alike in throngèd streets and deserts dim :
She never thought that there could be so bold
   A woman as to wish to comfort him.

If she could have imagined such a thing,
   So very unexpected, mean, and low,
That should with shame her sex's bosom wring,
   She had thought twice before she let him go.

THE ICE PRINCESS.

I am very sorry, but the only arrangement I
can make with regard to Theron is to marry
him. I should be compromised by any other.

Mamma would not hear of it. (*They move toward the iceberg.*)

MURIEL, *decisively.*

Very well, then, Theron cannot go with you.

THERON, *advancing.*

Yes, Muriel, I must go. I have always loved the princess. I shall marry her, and run the iceberg between New York and Liverpool in competition with the refrigerator-steamships for the transportation of Chicago beef. Now that I am engaged, my sole thought is to provide for my family; and in this I am sure all the gentlemen present will sympathize with me. I understand that the Ice Princess is an American fairy.

THE ICE PRINCESS.

I am. I was born in St. Louis.

THERON.

I thought I could not be mistaken in the accent. She will, therefore, be expensive.

CHORUS OF GENTLEMEN.

She will !

THERON.

But she will be worth the money.

CHORUS OF GENTLEMEN.

She will !

THERON.

Precisely. And for this reason I will explain
my new departure.

THERON, — *A New Departure.*

I am a family-man, —
A provident family-man !
And as a member of that great plutocracy,
Sprung from the heart of our New-World Democracy
I get all the money I can !

Formerly I was a youth,
Dreaming of Beauty and Truth,
Tender and hopeful, and somewhat æsthetical,
With an ideal both high and poetical.
(Perhaps it was *too* high in sooth !)

Now a more practical aim
I loudly and proudly proclaim;
And whether the prize you have drawn in love's
          lottery
Be of an origin earthly or watery,
          Yours I imagine the same.

I am a family-man, —
A provident family-man!
And as a member of that great plutocracy,
Sprung from the heart of our New-World Democracy,
          I get all the money I can!

MR. VANE.

Excuse me, Mr. Gay, but isn't this last song of yours rather too much like some of Gilbert and Sullivan's things?

THERON.

There *is* a slight resemblance. But, if the Princess intends to have me, she must have " Patience " with me.

CHORUS, *in great anguish.*

Oh !

STEWARD, *holding out his hand, still more enlarged.*

Don't forget the steward, sir !

THERON.

Have you change for a hundred-dollar bill?

STEWARD.

I could *keep* the change, sir!

THERON.

On second thoughts, I will send you an order
on the Treasurer of the Iceberg Transportation
Company. Well, Muriel, my former love, I must
say adieu, I suppose. The princess is getting
impatient. Good-morning. (*He bows distantly,
and gets over the rail on to the iceberg.*) Now,
love! (*He extends his hand toward the* PRINCESS,
who mounts the rail.) Will you jump, dearest?

THE ICE PRINCESS.

Into your arms, sweet!

THERON, *extending his arms.*

Well, then, darling! One, two, three! And
here you are! (*She leaps, and he catches her in
his arms. The fairies follow.*)

MURIEL, *hiding her face in her hands.*

Oh —h—h —h !

CHORUS OF ICE FAIRIES.

We who, till now, scarce knew that we were women,
  Perceive, each one, we always did adore
Some one among the passengers or seamen,
  And shall forevermore.

                    (*They return to the iceberg.*)

CHORUS OF GENTLEMEN PASSENGERS AND SEAMEN.

And we, who always knew that we were human,
  To our first, last, and only loves are true:
Never yet beings in the form of woman
  Attracted us, save you!   .

(*They cross the deck, as if to follow the fairies, while the*
  STEWARD *tries to collect his fees from them.*)

STEWARD.

Don't forget the steward, gentlemen !

MRS. VANE, *detaining* MR. VANE.

Matthew, don't you dare to speak to that nasty
queen of theirs !

MR. VANE, *freeing himself.*

My dear, the queen is ill, and in low spirits.
Besides, I have loved her from childhood.

MR. VANE, — *A Discovery.*

Ah, yes! unknown, unseen,
 And wholly unsuspected,
She was my bosom's queen,
 Adored, though undetected, —
Unknown, unseen,
 And wholly unsuspected!

Her image filled my breast
 With rapture and devotion;
Though, it must be confessed,
 I had not any notion
What filled my breast
 With rapture and devotion.

Around my path through life,
 Without the slightest warning,
My less and more than wife,
 She poured celestial morning, —
Around my life
 She poured celestial morning!

And now to her I go
    In spite of every danger:
I feel that I should know
    So intimate a stranger.
To her I go,
    In spite of every danger.

Farewell, O true and tried,
    And now at last forsaken!
I fancied you my bride,
    But find I was mistaken.
She was my bride,
    And I was quite mistaken.

    (*He gets over the ship's side on to the iceberg.*)

MURIEL.

Well, then, papa, if you must go, be good to
poor Theron! Theron, take care of papa!

MURIEL., — *An Adjuration.*

Be kind 'to each other!
    Whatever betide,
Your heart-burnings smother,
    Your enmities hide.

It seems to me I was going to say something
else. Oh, yes!

Be kind to each other!
  Be truthful, and be
Both father and brother
  Reciprocally.

No, that isn't it, either. Let me see : —

To your loved ones be tender
  At all times ; and, oh !
Endeavor to render
  A kiss for a blow.

It isn't in the least what I wanted to say ! I
was going to warn them against those horrid
things, and here I am actually encouraging them
to behave affectionately toward them ! I must
try again !

Be the harsh word unspoken,
  Upbraid not, nor chide :
For a frown oft has broken
  The heart of a bride.

What perfectly disgusting rubbish ! I don't
know where I could have got hold of it.

To those fond hearts and lonely
  Be husband and son
Together, but only
  Be careful which one.

It is getting worse and worse.   Really, it makes me sick !

> Look before, not behind, you!
>   For loves that are dead
> Let no vain sorrow blind you,
>   No vain tears be shed.

Why, how atrocious !   It is the most pessimistic thing I ever heard of !

> Then, away with remembrance,
>   Away with regret;
> Turn from Parting, Death's semblance,
>   Turn, live, and forget.

(*Bursting into tears.*)   Oh, dear !   The wrong words keep coming in spite of every thing. What shall I do?

MRS. VANE.

I know what *I* shall do.   Captain, I invoke, I demand, your protection.   Stop Mr. Vane !

CAPTAIN.

Stop him?   My dear madam, I am going myself.

CHORUS OF LADY PASSENGERS.

Is it thus, unkind commander
　Of the Mesopotam-i-a,
That you leave your ship to wander
　On the ocean as it may?
Is it thus that you abandon,
　Is it thus that you betray,
Us, without a glimpse of land on
　Either side? Stay with us, stay!

CAPTAIN.

No, ladies : under the circumstances I must
leave you. I have always loved one of these Iceberg Fairies. I don't know which, as yet. You
will be perfectly safe on the Mesopotamia. The
head-stewardess understands the working of the
ship ; and I have no doubt, that in a month, or
two months at the farthest, you will be in Liverpool. Although usually the last to leave the ship,
I shall leave it now, and leave it firmly.

CAPTAIN, — *An Advertisement.*

Though tempests drive the shuddering wreck
　Through the long night till morn,
The captain keeps the reeling deck
　To which his truth was sworn.

Though masts be toppled in the sea,
  Shrouds snapped, and canvas torn,
To his ship, as if his bride were she,
  He keeps the fealty sworn.

Woe if he falters! For the press
  Will hold him up to scorn
If he leave the ship in her distress,
  To which his truth was sworn.

But this is a wholly different case. The weather is good, the ship is in perfect trim; and I've no doubt you'll have a comfortable voyage. Mrs. Vane, will you kindly post this note for my former wife when you reach Liverpool? It informs her of the facts of this singular case.

MRS. VANE, *politely taking the letter.*

Certainly, captain: I shall be very glad.

CAPTAIN.

You are very kind.

  (*He gets over the ship's side upon the iceberg.*)

CHORUS OF PASSENGERS, *following him.*

We are lawyers and physicians,
Bankers, brokers, electricians,
Publishers, and politicians,

Russians, Polacks, Turks, Armenians,
Hindoos, Arabs, and Athenians,
Chinese, Japs, and Abyssinians,
Germans, Frenchmen, and Egyptians,
Orientals of all descriptions,
Editors, professors, students
Of all kinds, whom their imprudence
  In the mad pursuit of wealth,
Has compelled, for relaxation,
To endure a brief vacation,-
  Which we come to spend among you for our health.

(They rush up the slopes and peaks of the iceberg, and clasp
the ICE FAIRIES *in their arms.)*

CHORUS OF ICE FAIRIES.

Welcome, lawyers and physicians,
Bankers, brokers, electricians,
Publishers, and politicians,
Russians, Polacks, Turks, Armenians,
Hindoos, Arabs, and Athenians,
Chinese, Japs, and Abyssinians,
Germans, Frenchmen, and Egyptians,
Orientals of all descriptions,
Editors, professors, students
Of all kinds, whom your imprudence
  In the mad pursuit of wealth,

Has compelled, for relaxation,
To endure a brief vacation,
　　Welcome, welcome to our iceberg for your health!

(The seamen on the iceberg cast loose from the steamer, and they begin to drift apart, the CHORUS OF LADY PASSENGERS *thronging the rail, in tears.)*

CHORUS OF SEAMEN.

Dry your tears, little dears,
Left alone aboard the ship;
Needless all your anxious sighs;
Cease to pipe your pretty eyes!

We do not blame our lot,
Though we leave you on the ship:
With these hearts that love us, we,
Safe and merry all will be!

MURIEL.

And do I understand that you are really going off with that creature, Theron?

THERON.

Yes, Muriel, I am perfectly serious about it; that is, as serious as I can be under the circumstances. Of course I can't help smiling. I am very happy, but I am serious. The steward remains with you, and perhaps —

MURIEL, *in reproach.*

Oh, this from you, Theron ! (*To the* STEWARD, *sharply.*) You here, Robert? What are you doing? Why don't you go with the gentlemen?

STEWARD.

Well, miss, I 'ave a delicacy in statin' the true reason, miss —

MURIEL.

Poor Robert ! And do you *love* me, Robert?

STEWARD.

Yes, I have always loved you.

MURIEL.

And you are sure you're not actuated by any mercenary motive?

STEWARD.

Quite, miss.

MURIEL.

And you will always be kind to my poor, grass-widowed mother?

STEWARD.

Always, miss.

MURIEL.

Well! — But you would never be able to put on the ring with that ridiculous hand of yours!

STEWARD.

No, miss.   But I could take up the collection in it.

MURIEL.

True.   Well, then, take me, Robert!   But wait a moment till I bid poor Theron farewell.

MURIEL, — *A Despair.*

Ah, truant love! to whom I cannot send
  The broken heart I bear,
This cry I send, and would that I might wend
  As swiftly with it through the trackless air.

For, oh! so heavy, heavy, heavy lies
  Upon my soul some spell,
That on my lips, in mute eclipse,
  Trembles and faints the secret they would tell.

A formless cry I send athwart the deep,
   For none can help but you!
Nay, save me from the demon of my sleep!
   Come back, O love, come back! I love you too!

THERON, — *A Regret.*

O loved and lost! to whom I look and long,
   The deep yawns at our feet:
Wild memories throng, and tremble into song,
   On lips where once your kiss had been so sweet.

But never, never, never may I know
   Bliss once my soul's desire:
The flame sinks low that filled me with its glow,
   And nothing may revive the dying fire.

In vain you send your cry across the sea:
   For, if I would be true,
It is, you see, impossible for me;
   For her Imperial Highness loves me too!

CHORUS OF LADY PASSENGERS, *turning suddenly
upon* MURIEL, *who runs across the deck towards
the iceberg, and intercepting her.*

   Ah, heartless, fickle one!
   For you we are undone!
     If it had not been for you,
   All our husbands and our brothers,
   Sons, and very many others,
     Had continued true.

Now, what shall we do?
Follow! Catch her!
Seize her! Scratch her!
Fickle and untrue!

(*They pursue* MURIEL *round the deck: she flies, singing.*)

They will catch me!
Seize me! Scratch me!
Fickle and untrue!
Theron, love, I come to you!

(*She mounts the rail, and leaps after the iceberg, with a
shriek.*)

Ah — h — h !

(*The scene darkens till all is lost to sight, the* CHORUS
singing.)

Hush, hush,
Our Muriel raves!
Oh, cease your roar and rush,
Ye winds and waves!
Our Muriel raves!

A horrid anguish seems
To fill her dreams!
But from her dreams she breaks:
Our Muriel wakes!
Lo, Muriel wakes!

EPILOGUE.

(*The scene is gradually illumined again. MURIEL is dis-covered seated in her steamer-chair, as at the close of the first act; and every thing is restored to its former state.*)

THERON, *tenderly.*

Then, you *do* love me, Muriel?

MURIEL, *eagerly.*

Oh, *yes*, indeed! Where — where is the steward?

STEWARD.

'Ere I ham, miss.

MURIEL, *gasping.*

Well — well — ugh! Go away, please! No; show me your hand first. (*He shows it of its normal size and shape, and she examines it carefully.*) Why, I thought it had turned into a waiter!

STEWARD.

What waiter, miss?

MURIEL.

Oh, do go away! Where is the iceberg?

ALL.

What iceberg?

MURIEL.

And the fairies?

ALL.

What fairies?

MURIEL.

And that shameless princess?

ALL.

What shameless princess?

MURIEL.

But the ball? And the decorations? The flowers? The bow on Theron's back? And Carlino's? The Baby Grand piano? · And the refreshments?

ALL.

What ball, decorations. flowers, bow, piano, and refreshments?

MURIEL.

And the —

ALL.

What?

MURIEL., *with a sigh.*

Yes! I must have been dreaming.

THERON.

I thought you were dreaming, from a remark that you made.

MURIEL.

Don't — don't leave me, Theron.

THERON.

Never, Muriel, till the church has made you mine.

MURIEL.

But there are no clergymen on board.

CHORUS OF CLERGYMEN, *suddenly emerging from the crowd.*

Plenty ! Sore throat, you know !

(*They retire immediately.*)

MURIEL.

Well ! Don't you think you had better wait till after breakfast, Theron? I am quite faint.

THERON.

Perhaps I had.

MURIEL.

Papa !   •

MR. VANE.

Yes, my child?

MURIEL.

Shake hands with Theron.

MR. VANE, *complying.*

Yes, my child.

MURIEL.

Mamma !

MRS. VANE.

Yes, dear?

MURIEL.

Kiss Theron!

MRS. VANE, *obeying.*

Certainly, dear.

MURIEL.

Theron!

THERON.

Yes, love?

MURIEL.

Kiss — let me see! Oh, yes! (*By a sudden inspiration lifting the pug.*) Kiss Carlino!

THERON, *wildly embracing* MURIEL.

Oh, my love!

MURIEL.

Well, don't *eat* me, Theron, — at least, not till *I* have had something.

(*The breakfast-bell is heard from below.*)

THERON AND MURIEL, — *A Conclusion.*

THERON.

The breakfast-bell! The breakfast-bell!
It is the happy, happy sound,
That, at the hour which each knows well,
The whole huge hungry world goes round.
In keep and tower,
In hut and bower,
In street and wood, in field and fell,
We list the merry breakfast-bell.

CHORUS.

We list the merry breakfast-bell!

MURIEL.

The breakfast-bell! The breakfast-bell!
It rings for one, it rings for all.
On land or sea, if human, we
Obey its merry, merry call.
Fond love may burn,
And o'er her urn
The tears of sorrow rise and fall:
The breakfast-bell rings for us all!

CHORUS.

The breakfast-bell rings for us all!

(*They go out dancing,* — MURIEL *and* THERON *together,* MR. *and* MRS. VANE, *two maids, the* CAPTAIN *and* STEWARD, *and the* CHORUS OF PASSENGERS, *in couples. The* CHORUS OF SEAMEN *haul up a sail, and sing.*)

If I had a sweetheart, and she was a rover,
    Haul away, boys, haul away!
I'd follow her all the wide world over,
    Haul away, boys, haul away!

If she said yes, I never would leave her,
    Haul away, boys, haul away!
If she said no, I would go and grieve her,
    Haul away, boys, haul away!

For the will of a girl there is never any knowing,
    Haul away, boys, haul away!
She would want me to stay if she saw me going,
    Haul away, boys, haul away!

Then, never say die; keep a stiff upper lip, boys;
    Haul away, haul, haul away!
The wind is fair, and we've got a good ship, boys,
    Haul away, haul, haul away!

www.ingramcontent.com/pod-product-compliance
Lightning Source LLC
Chambersburg PA
CBHW030903050726
47500CB00009B/988